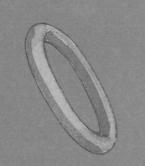

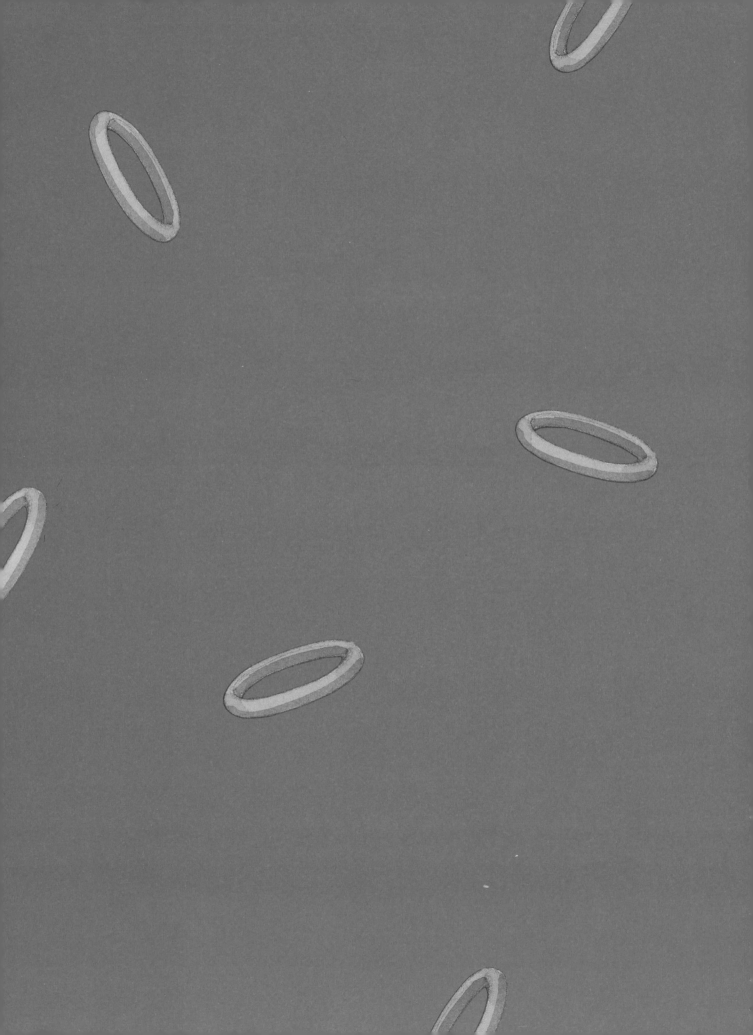

The 12 Days of Christmas

illustrated by

JERRY HARSTON

New York

On the first day of Christmas
My true love gave to me
A partridge in a pear tree.

On the second day of Christmas
My true love gave to me
Two turtledoves,
And a partridge in a pear tree.

On the third day of Christmas
My true love gave to me
Three French hens,
Two turtledoves,
And a partridge in a pear tree.

On the fourth day of Christmas
My true love gave to me
Four calling birds,
Three French hens,
Two turtledoves,
And a partridge in a pear tree.

On the fifth day of Christmas
My true love gave to me
Five golden rings!
Four calling birds,
Three French hens,
Two turtledoves,
And a partridge in a pear tree.

On the sixth day of Christmas
My true love gave to me
Six geese a-laying,
Five golden rings!
Four calling birds,
Three French hens,
Two turtledoves,
And a partridge in a pear tree.

On the seventh day of Christmas
My true love gave to me
Seven swans a-swimming,
Six geese a-laying,
Five golden rings!
Four calling birds,
Three French hens,
Two turtledoves,
And a partridge in a pear tree.

On the eighth day of Christmas
My true love gave to me
Eight maids a-milking,
Seven swans a-swimming,
Six geese a-laying,
Five golden rings!
Four calling birds,
Three French hens,
Two turtledoves,
And a partridge in a pear tree.

On the ninth day of Christmas
My true love gave to me
Nine drummers drumming,
Eight maids a-milking,
Seven swans a-swimming,
Six geese a-laying,
Five golden rings!
Four calling birds,
Three French hens,
Two turtledoves,
And a partridge in a pear tree.

On the tenth day of Christmas
My true love gave to me
Ten pipers piping,
Nine drummers drumming,
Eight maids a-milking,
Seven swans a-swimming,
Six geese a-laying,
Five golden rings!
Four calling birds,
Three French hens,
Two turtledoves,
And a partridge in a pear tree.

On the eleventh day of Christmas
My true love gave to me
Eleven ladies dancing,
Ten pipers piping,
Nine drummers drumming,
Eight maids a-milking,
Seven swans a-swimming,
Six geese a-laying,

Five golden rings!
Four calling birds,
Three French hens,
Two turtledoves,
And a partridge in a pear tree.

On the twelfth day of Christmas
My true love gave to me
Twelve lords a-leaping,
Eleven ladies dancing,
Ten pipers piping,
Nine drummers drumming,
Eight maids a-milking,
Seven swans a-swimming,
Six geese a-laying,

Five golden rings!
Four calling birds,
Three French hens,
Two turtledoves. . .

And a partridge in a pear tree.